T0078241

FIRST CAME
OUR COMPUTER CULTURE.
THEN CAME
THE SOCIETAL PHENOMENON KNOWN AS

. . . the geek.

Do you know someone who:

Consumes about ten cans of soda a day?

Camps out overnight for a ticket to
the new *Star Trek*® movie?

Rushes home on her lunch break to
get in an hour of *SimCity*™?

Hoards every piece of technical equipment
he has owned since childhood?

Considers the Macintosh vs. PC question to
have far-reaching religious consequences?

If the answer to any of these questions is **yes**,
then you're dealing with a geek. But don't worry.
THE GEEK HANDBOOK will help you not only
understand your geek's behavior but also
celebrate all the exciting features and
applications that geeks can offer.

User Guide and Documentation
for the Geek in Your Life

by Mikki Halpin

POCKET BOOKS

New York   London   Toronto   Sydney   Singapore

An *Original Publication* of POCKET BOOKS

 POCKET BOOKS, a division of Simon & Schuster Inc.
1230 Avenue of the Americas, New York, NY 10020

ISBN 978-0-671-03686-7

First Pocket Books trade paperback printing May 2000

10 9 8 7 6 5 4 3 2 1

POCKET and colophon are registered trademarks of Simon & Schuster Inc.

Cover illustration by pink design, inc.
Book design and illustration by Georgia Rucker/ pink design, inc.

Printed in the U.S.A.

this book is for
my mother
my friends
and
all the geeks in my life

Acknowledgments

Five years ago Victoria Manasserro Maat
and I wrote "A Girl's Guide to Geek Guys"
for our friend Noël Tolentino's zine
Bunnyhop. It was a humorous little essay
suggesting that women look beyond the
typical male to the underappreciated geek.
Little did we know that it would take on a
life of its own on the Internet through mailing lists, the Web, and the intervention of
HotWired. Last time I checked it was on
over 300 Web sites, in five languages.
Geeks love to read about themselves!
Thanks to Victoria, Noël, and Seth for that
initial inspiration—now maybe people will
believe me when I say I wrote it.

This book would not have been possible
without five amazing women: my agent,
Lydia Wills; my editor, Kim Kanner; and my
friends Marjorie Ingall, Georgia Rucker, and
Marcelle Karp.

Others who deserve thanks and praise are:
Katy Lain (xo), Jill McManus, the G-girls,
Halle und Eva, Wellington Fan, Jen Dalton,
Nicholas Butterworth, Sadie Plant, Gareth

Branwyn, Susannah McDonald, Dakota Smith, Anne Bray, Liz and Ingrid, Michelle and Robin, Lizanne Deliz, Andrea Juno, Danielle Claro, K-Neg, Peter and Lynette, Margie Borschke, Greg and Kim, Zelig, Cynthia Heimel, Darby Romeo, and my many friends both online and off. 6yb!

You can reach me at
www.thegeekhandbook.com

Contents

Chapter One: Getting Started *3*

   1.1 **The Conventions
Used in This Handbook**
*Why "your"
geek isn't really yours* *3*

   1.2 **How to Use This Handbook**
*Reference,
maintenance, troubleshooting* *5*

   1.3 **Do I Have a Geek?**
A helpful diagnostic *8*

   1.4 **You and Your Geek**
*The various models and
configurations. Features and tips* *11*

Chapter Two: Basics *23*

   2.1 **The Inner Geek**
*Understanding your
geek's emotional landscape* *23*

2.2 Communicating with Your Geek

The interpersonal infobahn 27

2.3 Geek-to-Geek Relations

How geeks behave in groups. The role of role-playing 34

2.4 Upgrading Your Geek

Encouraging your geek to perform more complicated tasks 45

Chapter Three: Maintenance 53

3.1 The Importance of Preventive Care

"Make the most of the container you've got" 53

3.2 Your Geek's Diet

Assessing your geek's dietary needs. Altering your geek's nutritional program 56

3.3 Your Geek's Cycles and Routines

Running on machine time, not biological 64

3.4 Your Geek's Moving Parts
*"A fit body is
more efficient, honey"* 71

**3.5 Common Geek Bugs and
Suggestions for Fixes**
Nip those nasty start-ups in the bud 79

Chapter Four: Living in a Geek World 93

4.1 Planning for the Future
Your geek's legacy 93

4.2 Your Geek's Lifespan
*Life extension and
risk management* 97

**4.3 Your Geek's Role in
the New Economy**
Life in a technocracy 102

4.4 Geek Values Go Global
*How geek culture
can change the world* 109

CHAPTER 1:
GETTING STARTED

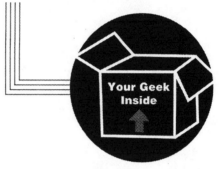

Your Geek Inside

1.1 The Conventions Used in This Handbook

The subtitle of this book is *User Guide and Documentation for the Geek in Your Life*. The term "user" is an artifact from other manuals of this type. Of course you don't want to think about "using" your geek, and "owning" or "operating" your geek doesn't sound much better. Geeks, more than anyone else, are their own people. A geek cannot be purchased, leased, or rented, although time-sharing is an option. Geeks are not available on the stock market (their companies are). When *The Geek Handbook* speaks of owners, it refers to anyone who has a relationship with a geek

"Your" geek is the geek who matters to you. Whether your geek is your boss, your parent, your child, your coworker, your lover, or your friend, you can improve the relationship by reading this book and understanding your responsibilities in the geek/nongeek dynamic. If you are baffled by the geek in your life or if your geek breaks down, you will gain many of the necessary skills to help your geek grow and thrive.

Historically, geeks have been feared and ostracized because they are containers of exotic, arcane knowledge unavailable to ordinary humans. Because of this persecution, many geeks have gone underground, often forming secret societies in order to pass on their rituals and codes. With the rise of computer culture, geeks are emerging from the shadows, and reengaging with mainstream culture. *The Geek Handbook* will help demystify your geek and allow you to better understand him or her.

1.2 How to Use This Handbook

Finally, full documentation is available for geeks and all their variations. In the same way that you use software manuals or guides to work with your computer, *The Geek Handbook* will help you to interact with your geek. Geeks are important assets and, properly maintained and modified, your geek can last well into the twenty-first century. Understanding your geek is a social skill no one can afford to do without. This handbook offers a competitive edge in an increasingly competitive world.

The handbook will provide step-by-step instructions for communicating with your geek, handy geek features, geek maintenance, and fixes for common geek bugs. Many geek behaviors are baffling, with no apparent evolutionary advantage. *The Geek Handbook* will explain these behaviors to you, help you cope with them, and, when necessary, provide suggestions for curbing them. (We call this "upgrading your geek.")

A geek spouse, parent or neighbor will easily be able to find such topics as "Your Geek's Diet" or "Grrr! The Hostile Geek." The dawn of the Geek Age is upon us, and the correct programming knowledge is essential. With proper use, *The Geek Handbook* can produce both immediate and long-term effects, resulting in healthier, happier geeks and owners. Even if you have experience dealing with geeks, *The Geek Handbook* will alert you to common geek bugs, and suggest both quick and long-term solutions. This handbook can significantly improve your geek's performance, and prepare you for any modifications the future holds.

The next chapter, Chapter Two, will give you general geek background, and some helpful tools for communicating with your geek. As you will see, there are features common to all geek models, but no two geeks are the same. It's important to use this handbook as a guide, not a blueprint. Individual variations are what make geeks unique and adaptable to so many applications. Spend time with your geek, get to know his or her history, and don't make changes just for the sake of change. Respect your geek.

Chapter Three is the core maintenance section of the handbook, with tips on keeping your geek healthy and at peak performance levels. Use this section to evaluate your geek, and to obtain the necessary skills that will help your geek lead a healthy, happy, and productive life.

Chapter Four looks at geeks in the world at large, and the way they are affecting (and affected by) global economics and social shifts. The final two sections of this chapter contain a diagnostic exercise and a guide to how geeks may enter your life.

1.3 Do I Have a Geek?

1. If you mention the Y2K bug he:

☐ a. Says he thinks Volkswagens are terrible cars.

☐ b. Proudly displays his food stock-pile, and explains that he has written a program which stalls all of the household chips in the last minute of 1999. After that date, time will cease to exist, but all of the computers will work.

2. When a new *Star Trek* movie opens she:

> a. Wonders if the franchise isn't played out.

> b. Has saved a place for you in line, because she camped out over night. During the movie, she gets really worked up when the crew in engineering does something with the warp core that she's *sure* isn't possible.

3. When playing Scrabble he:

> a. Forgoes actual competition to spell out cute things like *Kiss Me* and *Be Mine*.

> b. Keeps muttering that the on-line version is better and frequently consults his PDA, until finally admitting that he has pro-grammed it with an algorithm which prompts him with the most fruitful letter combinations. Uses words like "subroutine."

Answers

In each case, the answer b indicates a strong tendency toward geekiness. The more b answers, the more pure your particular geek is. If after taking this quiz you still aren't sure, read through the rest of the handbook for more clues.

Analysis

In question 1, your geek is trying to show you what a good provider he is. This is his retirement plan, his 401(k), his nest egg. If you want to gently suggest that the two of you address the Y2K issue in a different way, proceed with caution. Your geek has thought long and hard about this. He has carefully considered the options: a possible life without computers, as the millennium clock ticks over, or a life frozen in time, eternally 1999, but with all the computers working. He has chosen the latter. And he has already written the code. Asking him to change the plan is asking him to change the future. You might just want to resign yourself to the fact that at least you won't get any older.

In question 2, you are indeed loved if your geek will include you in her *Star Trek* experience. Treasure this time with her. If you cringe when she shouts out "Live long and prosper" you will gain nothing. Instead of pointing out that *none* of the technology on the *Enterprise* is real, so she couldn't really know the capacity of a dilithium crystal, ask her to explain further. Act interested.

In question 3, you have a highly socialized geek. Be happy that he will play analog Scrabble. Do not mock his geeky words.

1.4 You and Your Geek

Now that you know you have a geek, how does your geek function in your life? A few possibilities are outlined here, but what's important is that you study your own geek, and learn your geek's idiosyncrasies. While most geeks will have more in common with one another than they will with nongeeks, there are many variations on the basic model. Add this to the countless personae in the nongeek population, and the number of possible combinations is staggering. (As the Vulcans like to say, "Infinite Diversity in Infinite Combination.")

fig. 1.4.1 Your geek coworker

1.4.1 Your Geek Coworker

➕ *Features*

Everyone has a geek coworker. Even if you don't work in the tech industry, there's a geek or two somewhere in your organization, keeping the whole place up and running (in *their* eyes at least). These geeks are often the most underappreciated of all geeks, and they long for recognition of their role in whatever your company does, whether it's cosmetics shipping or UN translation services. Once you've wooed your geek coworker to your cause, there'll be no stopping you.

Known Bugs

They're often entranced by meaningless upgrades which will leave you unproductive for weeks. May be highly resistant to any suggestions of your own, and intolerant of idiosyncrasies. Your desire to use an Internet browser other than the one which your geek feels is morally and ethically correct counts as an idiosyncrasy.

Tip

Document, document, document. If you are able to tell your geek precisely what is wrong and to replicate the problem when you call for help, your geek will be extra motivated to help. He may attempt to bond further with you. Prepare to receive unasked for and unauthorized hardware, as well as lengthy expositions on the merits of proxy servers.

1.4.2 Your Geek Boss

Features

More and more geeks are ending up in management, taking on responsibilities for which they are ill-prepared. The geek boss has suddenly been tasked with coordinating the working processes of a group of high-performing eccentrics, when yesterday he was one of them. The geek boss is highly tolerant of offbeat working behaviors and will rarely ask you to neaten up your office or conform to any kind of dress code. He can be counted on to take the team out for a matinee on the day any good science fiction or action movie opens.

NOTE: attendance is mandatory.

Known Bugs

Looks at you with deep suspicion if you go home at a normal time, even if all he has been doing for the past five hours is playing *Diablo* and surfing through Slashdot and Linux Daily News. The worst bug will appear when your geek boss is called upon to enforce the status quo, a behavior deeply alien to his geek roots. He will not perform this task well and it will be you, the underling, who pays for his ambivalence. Just as you feign wild humor at his killer Bill Gates impression, you must also learn to look humble and appreciate his occasional rambling lectures. Don't point out that it's obviously taken from the management book he read on the plane.

Tip

Remember that geeks love to solve problems. There is nothing your geek boss will enjoy more than looking at something which has completely baffled you, immediately pointing to the problem, and outlining a solution. Use (or manufacture) these situations to engage with your geek boss and make him feel good about himself. But don't play too dumb—geek bosses have high expectations.

1.4.3 Your Geek Spouse or Lover

Features

Although the geek relationship does pose challenges in formation and in practice, it can be a very rewarding one for both parties. Geeks are loving and supportive partners, they can fix things, and they rarely stray. They love children and often share their interests. Watch your geek at the next family gathering: he'll head straight for the play room, especially if there are Legos involved. Geeks are open to interfaith marriages and generally won't rule you out for using a PC instead of a Mac or vice versa.

Known Bugs

Your friends may be taken aback initially. If fashion is important for you, think long and hard about dating a geek. Some mullets* are a badge of honor. Geeks have been known to date nongeeks for less than honorable reasons: a nongeek lover can provide many excuses for equipment purchases ("to get you up to speed") and are easily technically snowed.

Tip

You have to realize that the computer will be a vital presence in your relationship without allowing it to become a threat or a rival. Keep your *Geek Handbook* near, and learn to tune out your friends.

---

*The mullet is a classic geek hairstyle. Basically it means hair that is short in front and on the sides, while remaining rebel-length in back. Thus, it may symbolize the liminal role of the geek, crossing back and forth between corporate life and the hacker lifestyle. It is primarily found on the geek male, though feminine versions do exist. There is a strong anti-mullet segment of the geek population, which has only strengthened the resolve of those who still embrace the style.

1.4.4 Your Geek Parent

Features

There are few things as terrifying as the newly hatched geek parent. It's a two-stage development. In the first, or "tech support" phase, the parent will call frequently with such questions as "My printer is out of paper. What do I do?" In the second or "autopilot" phase, the parent develops his or her own netlife, and you will be left with a silent sense of foreboding, knowing they are out there somewhere. Phone calls decline as E-mails proliferate, including numerous virus alerts and the Neiman-Marcus cookie recipe.

Known Bugs

Stage Two often spirals out of control as the geek parent takes to forwarding lengthy cat haikus, URLs of their bingo web ring, and news of your high school nemesis. Keep an eye on parental daytrading.

Tip

Doing a search on your name in every major search engine before your geek parent figures them out can give you a leg up on explaining some of those Usenet posts you made in college. Putting up your own home page will give them hours of fun as they scour it for typos.

1.4.5 Your Geek Child

 Features

The parent of a geek child faces many challenges. You must honor your child's abilities and native culture, while preparing your young geek for a world which may mock and exploit him. The geek child will provide excellent tech support and has a high-paying career in store; he or she will rarely miss curfew, unless curfew includes turning off his machine.

 Known Bugs

Tendency to cracker rebelliousness may lead to criminal exploits. Parents often depend on the geek child for family finances and other technical chores, then are left in the lurch when the geek child leaves home for college or Seattle. Geek children have the irritating ability to research and debunk long-held family myths. Getting them to go on vacation can be a problem.

Tip

It's OK that your geek child never leaves the house. The successful parents of a geek child know when to urge social interaction and when to allow the geek child to withdraw. Those who provide refreshments and the necessary technology for LAN parties may find themselves extremely popular.

fig. 1.4.5 Your geek child

fig. 1.4.6 Your geek neighbor

1.4.6 Your Geek Neighbor

 Features

The geek neighbor is the most low maintenance geek. Your geek neighbor will have
all of the latest yard gadgets and satellite
hookups, and is eager to share this knowledge. Geek neighbors rarely travel (except
to cons and Comdex) and will happily watch
your house and feed your pets while you are
away. If you need ISDN or other tech solutions for your home office, stock up on soda
and invite your geek neighbor over.

Known Bugs

The geek neighbor's infatuation with technology can lead to unexpected civic

changes. Don't be surprised if you suddenly learn that your streets are being torn up for an experimental fiber-optic network.

Tip

Don't underestimate the geek neighbor as baby-sitter. As noted above, geeks share many of the interests of children and usually love to interact with them. Ordering a pizza and setting up a bowl of ooblick* in an easily cleaned area will keep your kids and your geek neighbor busy for hours.

---

*Ooblick is a mysterious substance that has long fascinated geeks. A mixture of cornstarch and water, it is a slimy, viscous medium with many odd physical properties. Make your ooblick in a big pan and encourage experimentation. The technical term "ooblick" is given in the *New Hacker's Dictionary v. 4.1.4*; however, many geeks refer to ooblick as "cornstarch and water."

CHAPTER 2:
BASICS

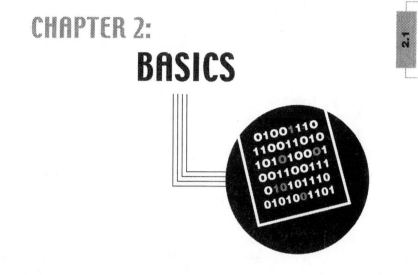

2.1 The Inner Geek

2.1.1 Your Geek and His Computer

You may find yourself comparing your relationship with your geek with the one you observe between your geek and his machine. Which of you does he spend more time with? Which one does he attend to more closely when it is broken? Which one does he buy things for? Which one does he brag about to his friends? Stop yourself right there. This way lies madness, or as your geek might put it, a nonproductive feedback loop. While there is always a certain tension between the geek's owner and the geek's computer,

fig. 2.1.1 Your geek and his computer

never ever let it develop into full-blown competition. Your geek's computer has always been there for him, every minute of every day and in no way do you want to come between the two of them.

Never view the computer as a rival. You don't want to make your geek have to choose or feel threatened. If there's one thing geeks have learned from playing *Doom*, it's to shoot first, ask questions later. Make sure your geek understands that when you encourage him to spend time away from the computer, it is not in order to win a victory for yourself. It is in order to help your geek feel more productive and happy when he is back at the computer. This is perhaps the most important lesson of *The Geek Handbook*.

2.1.2 Your Geek's Childhood

Like most humans, many of your geeks emotional schematics were formed in her childhood and early adulthood. Remember that her maturing experience may have radically differed from that of a nongeek. Representations of geeks in pop culture give us few clues as to what their inner societies are like, and anthropologists have been resistant to explore their culture.

Until a more in-depth field study can be made, you must interview your geek about his own experience. While the account your geek gives of his childhood may seem fanciful, it is important to remember that the distortions, if any, are as meaningful as the facts. Perhaps your geek didn't really have the idea for the Clapper™ when he was just seven or hook up his grade school to ARPANET, but you can rest assured that any adult geek of today was a bright, slightly unusual child, and very likely picked on by others.

Listen carefully to your geek. Despite any social awkwardness, did he do well in school? If so, your geek may be eager to please authority figures (or at least not hate them). Such a geek can thrive in a big business environment, but must be monitored so his superiors don't take advantage of his drive. Conversely, if your geek didn't do well in school, despite his brilliance, he may gravitate toward startups and fringe technologies. (See "Start-up Syndrome," section 3.5.2.)

Notice the sense of peace and excitement that drifts across your geek's face as he discusses his first geeky experiences. These references can be a clue to help you guide your geek to a happy and productive life. Does he talk more about the boxes and hardware or about the programs? If your geek tells you all about playing *Advent* and *M.U.L.E.*, his future may lie in game development. Or are there more references to the Atari 800, TRS 80, and the Apple IIe? You may have a hardware geek on your hands.

2.2 Communicating with Your Geek

Communication with your geek ought to be easy, right? After all, she's got three or four communication devices connected at any given time. But, just as computers need special cables and drivers in order to "talk" to one another, you will also need some special tools and skills in order to communicate with your geek.

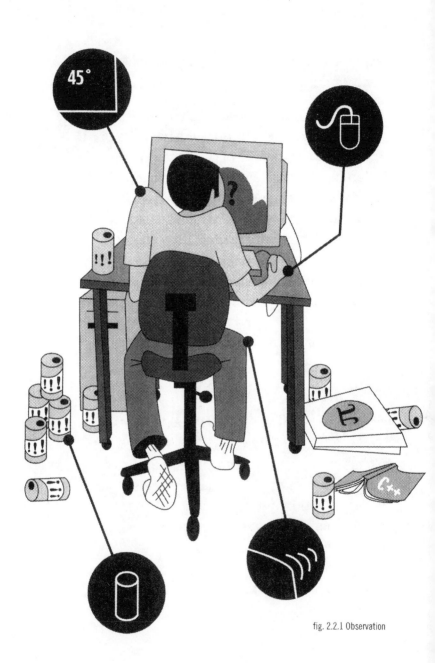

fig. 2.2.1 Observation

2.2.1 Observation (Visual Grep)

Traditional body language analysis doesn't work very well on geeks. It is usually based on a frontal view, and as you probably know by now, it is rare to see the full frontal geek until well into the relationship. You need to learn to analyze your geek from the back, unless you think you can catch his reflection in the monitor and go from there.

Physical Signals to look for:

Mouse grip

Is the mouse moving gracefully beneath the hand? Mouse clenching is a sure sign of geek stress. If your geek uses a trackball, check for white knuckles.

Degree of shoulder hunch

Tends to increase with concentration. Try to examine your geek in various moods and check to see his ear-shoulder ratio in each. Soon you will be able to tell at a glance how his day is going.

> *Shoulder straight or sloping downward:*
> Your geek is normal.
>
> *45° angle:* Your geek is alert and happy.

>45° angle: Your geek is experiencing stress, but may be enjoying it.

Shoulders near or touching ears: Your geek is in overload. Tell him to Ctrl-c out of there.

Variety and depth of spoor

Of course "normal" refuse level varies from geek to geek. This is merely a guideline.

1–10 soda cans: Normal day.

10–20 soda cans, plus pizza boxes: Low to medium stress.

Not sure where geek or desk is: High stress, near deadline, suggest you tiptoe away.

Leg Jiggling

Zero: Your geek may be frozen.

10–60 bpm: Your geek is in a deep programming state. He may also be timing things.

60–100 bpm: Your geek is attempting to relieve stress and pent-up energy.

> This is a good time to suggest a walk.
> If you have to, suggest a walk to Fry's.

Away from the machine, your geek's body language may be deceptive. She may present as uncomfortable, cranky. This is not directed at you. This is because she has nothing to do. She is insecure because she is away from her machine. This anxiety can become gripping at times, and may cause an otherwise emotionally at-peace geek to lash out.

If you want to talk to your geek, or spend some quiet off-line time with her, consider providing a low-intensity activity for her during these sessions. A jigsaw puzzle or some Legos can be very helpful. Remember to monitor your geek carefully for obsessiveness: if she begins building a robot with the Legos, take them away and substitute a more organic project. Sorting things or washing dishes both work well.

If you fear your geek may be tronning (going so deeply into machine space that she is unreachable), execute a priority interrupt. Methods for a priority interrupt vary: Some geeks respond to loud noises, others don't.

It's best to have a prearranged signal with your geek for such emergencies.

2.2.2 *Star Trek* as Interpretive Tool

 Joseph Campbell wrote that you can understand a culture's values by studying its heroes. This is true of geek culture as well. One character in particular is resonant with geek ideals and dreams. His name is Data, and he is an android. Because he is at once the ultimate human and the ultimate machine, it is unclear at this time whether most geeks wish to *be* Data, or just hang out with him.

Look at the chart on the facing page. On the left, you'll see what your geek admires about Data. On the right, you'll see what this tells you about your geek. You see here why you need the handbook. It is not enough to know that Data is a character on *Star Trek: The Next Generation*. It is not enough to know that he is an android. You need special interpretive skills to discern Data's significance in the geeky scheme of things. Put this chart on your wall and consult it frequently.

Some of Data's key characteristics, and what they can teach you about your geek:

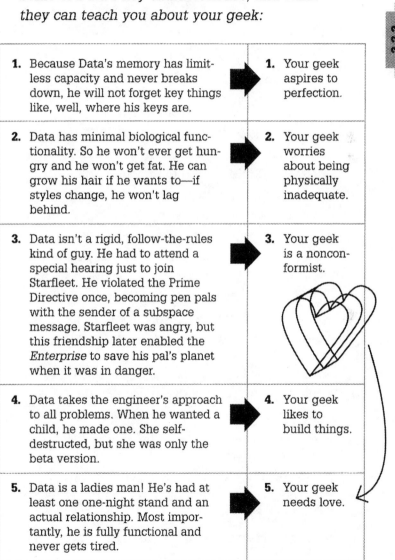

1. Because Data's memory has limitless capacity and never breaks down, he will not forget key things like, well, where his keys are.	**1.** Your geek aspires to perfection.
2. Data has minimal biological functionality. So he won't ever get hungry and he won't get fat. He can grow his hair if he wants to—if styles change, he won't lag behind.	**2.** Your geek worries about being physically inadequate.
3. Data isn't a rigid, follow-the-rules kind of guy. He had to attend a special hearing just to join Starfleet. He violated the Prime Directive once, becoming pen pals with the sender of a subspace message. Starfleet was angry, but this friendship later enabled the *Enterprise* to save his pal's planet when it was in danger.	**3.** Your geek is a nonconformist.
4. Data takes the engineer's approach to all problems. When he wanted a child, he made one. She self-destructed, but she was only the beta version.	**4.** Your geek likes to build things.
5. Data is a ladies man! He's had at least one one-night stand and an actual relationship. Most importantly, he is fully functional and never gets tired.	**5.** Your geek needs love.

2.3 Geek-to-Geek Relations

2.3.1 Your Geek and His Friends

Though geeks are often loners, they nonetheless have a network of relationships which perform social functions. A node might include coworkers, former college programming mates, role-playing-game colleagues, or fellow special effects enthusiasts. The geek friendship is often attenuated—though a geek may know a friend's coding idiosyncrasies and wax wroth about a pal's Playstation prowess, your geek will rarely know where his fellow geeks live. (He may know their IP addresses.)

It's best to allow your geek to maintain these relationships on his own. You can be assured that the time he spends with his friends is productive; geeks bond during shared activities such as work, fan culture and narrative card games. (These activities are sometimes referred to as "cluster-geeking.") This will give you plenty of space for your own projects. If you fear your geek and his friends aren't getting any fresh air at all, try to think of an off-line activity they might enjoy. Something with a sense of purpose will make them happy: visiting the Air and Space Museum or a trade show will give them the "flow" they need.

2.3.2 Geeks and History

While a comprehensive geek history has yet to be written, it is helpful to be aware of some key moments in the evolution of geek culture. Your geek feels that she is a part of a continuum of geek culture, and you should respect that.

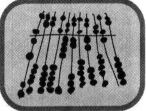

The dust abacus

3000 B.C.E. An unnamed Babylonian invents the dust abacus (basically a flat surface with pebbles or chunks of dirt representing numerical values). Truly working with the materials at hand, this geek pioneer revolutionized calculation and began a move toward a numerical language. (The bead and wire abacus didn't come along until 500 B.C.E., in Egypt.)

900 B.C.E. Muhammad ibn Musa al-Khwarizmi, a Tashkent cleric, writes out the first algorithm and introduces the concept of mathematical abstraction. It is unknown if he solved for x or for y.

1614 C.E. Scotsman John Napier discovers logarithms. Napier also attempted to build a "death ray" using mirrors, sunlight, and various lenses. Both his interests live on, one as a mathematical principle, the other a reliable option for villains in Bond movies.

1623 C.E. Wilhelm Schickard, a German mathematician and cleric, builds his "calculator-clock." The device is similar to a slide rule.

Calculator–clock

1633 C.E. The astronomer, mathematician, and physicist Galileo Galilei is tried by the Catholic Inquisition for supporting the Copernican theory that the earth revolves around the sun. While Galileo did renounce his beliefs under duress, his is an extreme object lesson of the persecution many geeks suffer at the hands of the status quo. Geeks rejoiced when the Vatican officially struck down its own prohibition in 1992 and exonerated Galileo. (Geek attitudes toward religion vary, but vindication is always nice.)

1642 C.E. Blaise Pascal develops his "numerical wheel calculator" and grandiously names it "Pascaline." Previously Pascal had derived a hydraulic principle known as Pascal's Law. Pascal's hubris is rewarded in 1967 when Niklaus Wirth names a new (and often derided*) programming language for him.

1646 C.E. First known use of the word "computer" in English. Sir Thomas Browne uses it to refer to those who calculate time in the process of creating calendars. (Your geek probably doesn't have much use for calendars; see Section 3.3.1, "How Your Geek Experiences Time.")

---

*See "Why Pascal is Not My Favorite Programming Language," by Brian Kernighan (in *Comparing and Assessing Programming Languages*) or "Real Programmers Don't Use Pascal" by Ed Post (originally published in *Datamation*).

1752 C.E. Benjamin Franklin ties a key to a kite and flies it during a storm in order to prove that lightning is electricity. Franklin has cred for geek extremism and inventiveness, but his policy of "a penny saved is a penny earned" would not have won him many defense contracts.

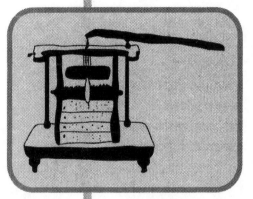

Loom with cards

1805 C.E. Joseph-Marie Jacquard develops a system which will allow perforated cards to run looms in textile factories. Riots occur as the specter of machines replacing manpower is first raised.

1823 C.E. Charles Babbage receives what may have been the first government grant, £1,500 from the British government in order to finance his "Difference Engine." Despite ten years of work and additional grants totalling £17,000, the machine was never built.

(A near perfect copy was produced in the 1990s as a showpiece.)

1833 C.E. Babbage begins work on the more ambitious "Analytical Engine."

1842 C.E. Augusta Ada King (née Byran), Countess of Lovelace, documents Babbage's work and programs the Analytical Engine. A significant milestone, because Babbage's ideas didn't propagate until she distributed his notes, and also because Lovelace is generally referenced when geek culture is accused of sexism.

1884 C.E. Nikola Tesla arrives in America. He goes on to pioneer innovations in radio, electric current, vacuum tubes, and many other areas. Germ-phobic and really geeky (at dinner parties he often calculated the cubic contents of his plate), Tesla set a standard for brilliance and eccentricity which still stands.

1890 C.E. Herman Hollerith uses a punched card tabulating machine to process the data from the 1890 U.S. Government Census. Hollerith's

Tabulating Machine Company, after several mergers, will eventually become IBM.

1924 C.E. Thomas J. Watson, Sr. becomes CEO of the Computing-Tabulating-Recording Company, a descendant of Herman Hollerith's 1880 venture and changes its name to IBM (International Business Machines) to better represent a new focus on data-processing services. Watson wasn't a geek, but a sharp businessman who saw their economic potential. He made IBM attractive to geeks with a large research and development budget, an easy-to-understand dress code, and the promise of lifetime employment.

1936–1937 C.E. Alan M. Turing develops the idea of a computational machine which will perform a specific set of functions. Though the "Universal Machine" remained theoretical, the Turing specifications become an industry standard. Perhaps the first known

Hollerith card

Person
Native
White   Foreign
Male   Colored
Age 0   Female
    1   0
    2   1

instance of marketing outpacing technology. (Turing also theorized the "Turing Test," a standard for artifical intelligence.)

1939 C.E. First Radio Shack catalog is published.

1945 C.E. Grace Murray Hopper reports a "bug" while working on the Mark I Computer at Harvard University and begins "debugging." The terms were in existence prior to this, perhaps as early as 1878, but this is thought to be the first time they are applied to a computer. The term "project deadline extension" probably comes into use soon after.

Cover of first Radio Shack catalog

1946 C.E. The ENIAC (Electronic Numerical Integrator and Computer) is dedicated. A quote from the press release, "It is capable of solving many technical and scientific problems so complex and difficult that all previous

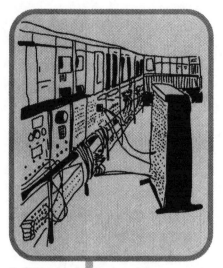

The ENIAC

methods of solution were considered impractical."

1949 C.E. The Whirlwind I, the first digital computer, boots up at MIT. It takes up 3,300 square feet, distributed over two floors.

1952 C.E. With a dummy console in the studio and the actual processor in Philadelphia, a UNIVAC I used by the network CBS correctly predicts that Eisenhower will win the election, based on 7 percent of the votes. However, CBS mistrusts the results and waits until the next day to run the news.

1952 C.E. University of Wisconsin Press publishes the first computer manual, the imaginatively titled *Computer Manual*, by Fred Gruenberger.

1958 C.E. Congress, fearful of losing the space race to the Soviets, funds ARPA (Advanced Research Projects Agency) with a $520 million appropriation. ARPA, under J.C.R. Licklider, funded time-sharing research which directly led to network development, and supported the first Ph.D. programs in computer science.

1963 C.E. ASCII is established.

1968 C.E. Doug Engelbart demonstrates a keyboard attachment to his colleagues at SRI. About twenty years later, the "mouse" device is made available to consumers on the Apple Macintosh. Engelbart also contributed to the Xerox Alto (1973), the first computer designed to be connected to a network.

1969 C.E. Unix, the quintessential geek operating system, is born at Bell Laboratories.

1970 C.E. Xerox PARC is founded.

1972 C.E. Pong is released.

1974 – 1975 C.E. The Altair 8800 and 680 hit the market. Named for a planet on an episode of *Star Trek*, the Altair

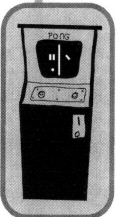

Pong

was available in kit form for $345 and launched the dream of a computer in every home. One of the first interpreters for the Altair was written by future tycoons Paul Allen and Bill Gates.

1980 C.E. The number of computers in the world reaches one million.

1982 C.E. *Time* magazine picks the computer as "Man of the Year." Author William Gibson coins the term "cyberspace."

1982 C.E. Apple becomes the first personal computer company to reach a one billion dollars annual sales rate. The company's founders, Steve Jobs and Steve Wozniak, first went into business together in their teens, producing a blue box that allowed the user to make free, illegal long distance calls.

1984 C.E. Apple releases the first Macintosh.

1986 C.E. Microsoft goes public. Geeks

begin to realize their role in the global economy.

1990 C.E. The "World Wide Web" internet protocol is created at CERN, a Swiss research institution.

1991 C.E. The National Science Foundation lifts restrictions against commercial use of the internet. The Geek Age begins.

2.4 Upgrading Your Geek

2.4.1 Define the Problem for Your Geek

Begin by programming your geek to perform simple tasks. Let's say you want him to finally get the air conditioner working. It's hot, and the only thing that is going to make you happy is a nicely chilled house and some ice cream. You look over at your geek, who is typing away, oblivious to both the heat and your needs.

Don't expect your geek to figure out what you want all by himself. Dropping hints that even an ordinary human might miss will get you nowhere. Consider the examples below. Example 1a is what you hope will happen.

Example 1a

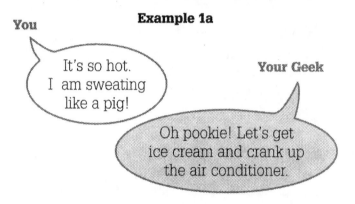

You

It's so hot. I am sweating like a pig!

Your Geek

Oh pookie! Let's get ice cream and crank up the air conditioner.

Example 1b is what will happen.

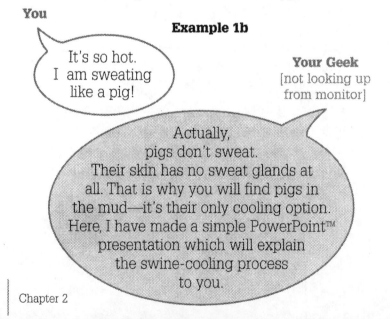

You

Example 1b

It's so hot. I am sweating like a pig!

Your Geek
[not looking up from monitor]

Actually, pigs don't sweat. Their skin has no sweat glands at all. That is why you will find pigs in the mud—it's their only cooling option. Here, I have made a simple PowerPoint™ presentation which will explain the swine-cooling process to you.

It's not that your geek lacks sympathy—he cares about you. It is just that he cannot process the information you are presenting, so he is focusing on a flaw in your data. Strange as it may seem, he is debugging you to get the program to work. Geeks have learned to be very precise in pinpointing and analyzing problems. Once you know this, it will be easier to frame your comments so as to get a more desirable outcome, as seen in Example 1c.

You   **Example 1c**

It's so hot. I wonder
if it is possible to put the air
conditioner on a timer so that it will
be cool when we get home
from work.

Your Geek

Where's
my toolbox?

It's here!
I'll go get the
ice cream.

You

Or consider this scenario. Example 2a is your intended result.

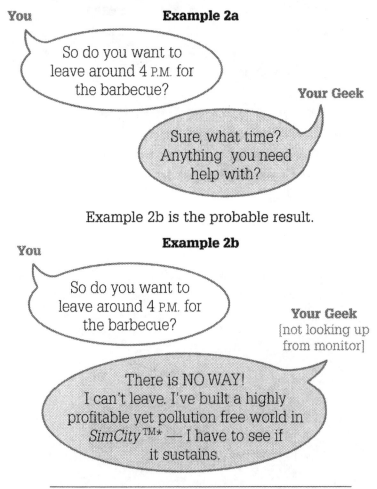

You

Example 2a

So do you want to leave around 4 P.M. for the barbecue?

Your Geek

Sure, what time? Anything you need help with?

Example 2b is the probable result.

You

Example 2b

So do you want to leave around 4 P.M. for the barbecue?

Your Geek
[not looking up from monitor]

There is NO WAY!
I can't leave. I've built a highly profitable yet pollution free world in *SimCity* ™* — I have to see if it sustains.

---

*Originally released in 1989 and still going strong in endless new configurations, *SimCity*™ is a game environment which allows users to design, build, and rule a city of their dreams. Variables include crime levels, pollution, poverty, urban development, and taxation rates. Though *SimCity*™ technically doesn't have a win/lose outcome, the game nonetheless appeals to the geeky megalomaniac streak. It is an evil genius fantasy in a box.

Your geek knows that social interaction is important (especially if you've been using the handbook). But your geek also believes in helping as many people at once as possible, and your geek knows the predictive value of science fiction. A successful utopian game scenario could somehow spur a scientific and ethical breakthrough down the line one day, as well as providing significant boasting rights. She can't abandon that for a barbecue. Keeping this in mind, show your geek that the party also offers an opportunity to help people and show off. See example 2c.

Example 2c

You

This is going to be so fun. I hear they have one of those grills based on NASA technology, and the flame is very strong, while being wholly contained in a vacuum tube or something. I'm not totally clear.

Your Geek

There is NO WAY! A flame can't exist in a vacuum. I had better go over there and explain how they got duped. Are you ready to go?

2.4.2 Common Missteps

Don't view the upgrade process as a conversation: Your geek doesn't. Your geek regards conversation as a primitive way of exchanging information, and may be lost when you expect intuitive responses. By being aware of this, and tailoring your side of the conversation so that your geek understands what is expected of him, you can get the results you want.

Your geek may become recalcitrant and refuse to accept the fun challenge you have presented. When your geek says that your desired configuration, programming need, or access problem cannot be achieved, he is probably only testing you. Perhaps you have failed to show proper appreciation for your geek's achievements in the past? When your geek balks, do not become angry. Remember to present it as an intellectual question the two of you are considering together. Say things like "is there a workaround?" Depersonalize the issue.

Sometimes it is necessary to "go cowboy" on your geek and bring things to a standoff. When your geek blandly tells you that something isn't possible, thank him for his time. Suggest that he is clearly very busy, and that you will attempt to solve the problem yourself. Tell your geek you will need root access for this, and demand all passwords necessary. Ask where the Camel Book* is. Your geek will immediately and grumblingly do what you need him to do. Act impressed and grateful.

*The reference book *Programming Perl* has an image of a camel on its cover.

CHAPTER 3:
MAINTENANCE

3.1 The Importance of Preventive Care

It is essential that you keep your geek in top condition. It won't be easy. Many geeks are proud of their lack of physical health, as they consider themselves to be cerebral beings who function beyond the demands of physical bodies. The geek fantasy of future life as a cyborg or even a head in a jar points to a longing for a time when physical breakdown is unlikely, and easily repaired. "Who cares if a little piece snaps off?" your geek will think. "They can fix it in sickbay."

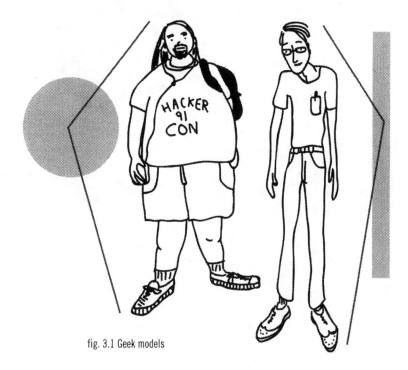

fig. 3.1 Geek models

Geeks come in two general models: fat geeks and skinny geeks. Guessing which one your geek is should be fairly easy, but even skinny geeks must be monitored for weight gain, due to sedentary lifestyle and poor nutrition.

You need to gently train your geek to monitor his own health, and to take a few simple proactive steps to ensure longevity. Remind your geek that Stephen Hawking represents a medical miracle and not a role model. Suggest that your geek run a self-diagnostic. If the results come back indicating some lifestyle changes are in order, look sympathetic and be ready to help. Emphasize that you love his mind AND its container and that you know his superior mindpower can conquer any silly bad habits he may have fallen into.

Even the most recalcitrant geek can become healthier, but expect these issues to continue to flare up, no matter how reformed your geek appears. Stay firm. However, if your geek begins referring to himself as "the resistance," some negotiation may be in order. When enthusiasm flags, tell your geek that you don't have a backup program. He's the only geek you've got and you want him around for a long time.

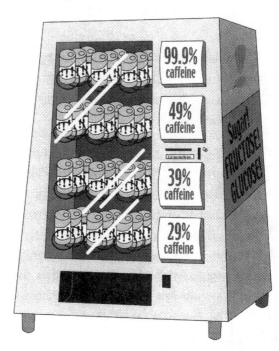

fig. 3.2.1 Food as fuel

3.2 Your Geek's Diet

3.2.1 Food as Fuel

As in all things, geek eating is geared toward maximum efficiency. Favored geek foods are high in calories and/or caffeine. Look around your geek's computer to see what his recent diet has been. You are likely to find fast food wrappers, vending machine detritus, and plenty of soda containers. And again, check the future. Captain Picard's French ancestry aside, you don't see a lot of gourmet meals eaten in space.

There is an old programming adage called

GIGO,
or
"garbage in garbage out."

It holds that a program is only as good as the data that is entered into it—even flawlessly written code will produce bad results if you feed it bad info. The same goes for your geek! If you explain to your geek that he will have better stamina and more energy by improving his diet, he may be gently coaxed into a more normal regimen, though we cannot expect miracles.

3.2.2 Food as Fun

A good way to ease your geek into healthier, more omnivorous eating habits is to encourage his love of the exotic. Your geek may not eat alien food in his lifetime, but he can sample the tastes of many cultures. Even if it means leaving work to eat, he'll have the opportunity to boast the next day that snails, ants, or other impressive items have been consumed. Foods that are eaten in unusual ways, such as Indian dipping breads, or in unusual settings (the planetarium?) also appeal to the geek. The eating experience should be as interactive as possible for your geek to enjoy it, but be careful not to overload your geek.

Suprisingly, geeks are not interested in the so-called space foods of the 1970s and their descendants, the sports drinks and bars of today. Oh sure, your geek might enjoy a Tang now and then for a retro fun thing, but remember, your geek was more interested in the rockets than in the astronaut lifestyle. Plus, Tang has no caffeine. Geeks on the west coast may enjoy "boosted" juice drinks which are blends of juice and ginseng, kava, gingko, etc.

Ease your geek into foodstuffs that aren't premade. Remind him that recipes can be found on-line, but encourage him to come up with his own "equations." If your geek leans toward the chemistry or biology side of geekdom, food science may be an exciting topic for him. Let your geek lovingly explain to you why the flour makes the gravy thicken, and why you should add salt to boiling water. Caution: don't encourage this too much, or your kitchen may be turned into a laboratory. See microwave note below.

Help your geek learn to love the processes of food preparation. Don't forget the importance of gadgets. Until there's a replicator in every household, there are an infinite number of appliances which will fascinate your geek. Do you think your geek won't want a hard-boiled egg slicer? You would be wrong. You have probably already noticed that the microwave holds great attraction for your geek as an experimental device. If he seems more prone to Peep races* than to culinary pursuits, get an extra appliance for the garage.

3.2.3 Eating at Home with Your Geek

Some owners mistakenly assume that a geek who feels connected to her machine would want to eat away from the keyboard. This is wrong. Part of the relationship between your

---

*"Peep races" involve marshmallow peep candy, a microwave or two, and a timer. You get the picture.

geek and her machine is that to her, there isn't so much of a divide between the two. Your geek enjoys sitting at the keyboard, and eating a slice, imagining that she is rejuvenating and repowering both herself and her PC. In this world view, crumbs and drips on the keyboard are merely an extension of a happy symbiotic relationship. Introduction of biological matter into the system can also provide a great excuse to upgrade. Remember, it's not your problem if she gets crumbs in her machine—let her deal with it. Your concern is what is going into her mouth. Put some carrot and celery sticks near the desk and put the chips just out of reach.

Sometimes, of course, you are going to want your geek to actually sit at the dining-room or kitchen table. A table without even a laptop on it. Gently ease your geek into eating away from the machine, first by arranging meals in the same room as the computer, with the computer still on. Then move gradually to meals with the computer off, until your geek can actually make it through an entire meal in a separate room without leaping up to check E-mail, see what the temperature is in Canada, or checking the Coke machine webcam at CERN.

3.2.4 Eating Out with Your Geek

Occasionally you may attempt to take your
geek off-site for a dining experience. A meal
off the grid presents several challenges. Try
incorporating your geek's surfing skills into
the planning. Say to your geek "I wonder if
there is a Moroccan restaurant near the
movie theater, with parking, and entrées
between twelve and fifteen dollars?" Your
geek will happily hunt down this information
for you on various city guides and search
engines, while the phone books of your
father's generation sit sullenly. Warning: this
option does limit you to eating at places in
the search engines, but at least you're getting out of the house.

Ready to go? Your geek will arm himself
with a palmtop, cellphone, GPS, beeper, and
anything else he can think of. Your nice meal
at a local bistro has turned into an Apollo
mission. There are two ways to confront
this. One is to go to a geek-themed restaurant which provides an arcade or other stim-
ulating environment. He won't need his
silicon security blanket if you give him a roll
of quarters. The other strategy is to appeal
to your geek's rebel side. There is a moment

in many geek narratives where the hero is required to go forth with no technology to help him. Remember, the Federation always ultimately beat the Borg with nothing but their human ingenuity even when all shields were down. Carelessly say to your geek that you know some programmers need those silly accouterments, but you know that your geek is so efficient that they aren't necessary. Besides, surely if the server goes down, either the company will send out a SWAT team for him, or he will *just know*. It is like a mother hearing her baby cry.

Occasionally your geek may be required to go to formal functions. Whether he is nominated for an award in the cutthroat field of fontography, attending a product launch, or having dinner with the new CIO, the prospect of eating with utensils in public is likely to throw your geek into a tizzy. Suggesting a practice meal or even etiquette lessons beforehand can result in a calmer, less babbling geek. Hoarding (see section 3.5.1) can kick into gear when your geek sees a fancy buffet table. Don't be surprised if you catch your geek stuffing canapés and other weird foods he would never eat into the pockets of his ill-fitting suit. Gently lead your geek away from the food and ask him to introduce you to the members of his team. They will be the ones in the corner seeing if they can hack into the sound system.

3.2.5 Programming Fluid

Geeks like sodas. Soda is an effervescent friend who delivers both sugar and caffeine. Despite advertising that associates soft drinks with tanned, athletic, outdoorsy consumers, geeks feel strongly that a canned beverage consisting mainly of chemicals is their drink of destiny. (Clearly the soft drink industry hasn't yet discovered geeksploitation; see section 4.3.3.) Soda consumption is a competitive activity, and every machine room has a "champ" whose pile of cans looms over all the others.

Soda may be the most difficult junk food from which to wean your geek. J.C.R. Licklider, the influential author of *Man-Computer Symbiosis* and an internet pioneer, is said to have begun every day with a cola. Try providing your geek with some URLs which discuss the hazards of high soda intake and see if he cuts down on his own. If he doesn't, encourage seltzer as a substitute (still fizzy; no chemicals, sugar, or caffeine). As a desperate strategy, spilling a soda on a beloved machine can get them banned from the tech room. Proceed with caution.

3.3 Your Geek's Cycles and Routines

3.3.1 How Your Geek Experiences Time

It's not the way the rest of us do. Geeks *process* their time, sometimes slowly, sometimes quickly, but always according to their internal drives. Man-made markers (especially those tied to nature such as A.M. and P.M., daylight savings, etc.) mean little to the geek in his world.

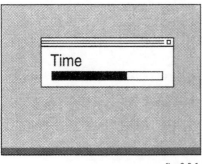

fig. 3.3.1

Time zones also mean little to the geek, who can E-mail anyone at any moment.

This is not to say geeks are immune to time. Geeks care about history, and they hate to see time wasted. Anyone who has seen her geek freak out in a checkout line knows this. What gets your geek going? It's not so much time as the inefficiency of the retail checkout process that is a hot button. Why, your geek wonders, do we put the items in a container, dump them *out* of the container, swipe them across the scanner and then put them in another container? Your geek may experience meltdown as he considers the sloppy flowchart which produced this time-consuming system. Remember, geeks pioneered mail order for all of their software and hardware needs. Look at how a geek internet shopping site is designed. You put items in your basket, and then one click later they are on their way to you. There is no clerk, there is no slowly moving treadmill of consumer items. Face-to-face interaction has been eliminated in favor of a more pure transaction.

We know from the timeline in section 2.3.2 that chronology is important to geeks. What happened in 1975? The Altair was on the cover of *Popular Mechanics* and the PC revolution began. But while the scientific record is immutable, don't expect your geek to remember things like birthdays, dinner times, anniversaries, and when your child is due home from school. This is what beeping watches, pages, and other devices are meant for. When a little machine tells your geek something should be done, he will do it. His sense of immediacy will make up for his sense of history every time.

Geeks often set their inner clock around a date, particularly dates tied to the software market. When you experience your geek's phase changes as random, it may be due to faulty information sharing regarding your geek's worklife. Remember that your geek may not set the dates for her own projects— the morons in management or marketing probably do this for her. But if you coax your geek and cultivate friends in other departments, you may be able to find out in advance when any crunch times might be occurring. Foreseeable crunch times, that is.

3.3.2 Is Your Geek Nocturnal?

While seemingly immune to the planets' movements, many geeks default to being

night people and love to function noctur-
nally. In olden days (the early to mid eight-
ies) many geeks had to practically live in the
computer lab in order to get access to
machines for their coursework. Large
machines like VAX and Cray supercomput-
ers functioned as a sort of communal hearth,
and may have provided your geek with his
first great peer-bonding experience. Every
time he burns the
midnight oil, your
geek remembers his
first nights in with
the guys.

fig. 3.3.2

Your geek will argue
that many scientific
and engineering
breakthroughs occur
completely through fortuitous accident. The
geek theorizes that the more time he spends
at work, the more he maximizes his chances
of such a breakthrough occurring. It is a logic
that is hard to argue with. Donald Watts
Davies and Paul Baran, working independently and unknown to one another, devel-
oped the packet switching protocol on which
the internet is based nearly simultaneously

in 1970. Having missed the chance to get in on this, your geek won't want to sleep through the next opportunity.

There aren't many ways to get around this deep geek belief that long hours bring big rewards, even if they aren't productive hours. You can try asking your geek to think about serendipity from a distribution standpoint. If inspiration is *truly* random, then it could occur anywhere, and lengthy stints at the desk won't necessarily increase the chance of it hitting, right? However, it's likely your geek will either see through this and argue that a prepared mind is more receptive to breakthroughs, or begin a lifelong research program about the statistical breakdown of original thought, and you've compounded the problem.

3.3.3 How Your Geek Manages Time

As in all things, your geek needs to learn a little bit about moderation. All-nighters are appropriate in cases of emergency or wild inspiration. Hoping for inspiration or stealing code on-line do not count. Remind your geek that he needs to save his creative juices for more important events, so that he has resources available when they do come up.

Geeks often feel the need to stay up in solidarity with a colleague, perhaps quietly playing *Half-Life* in an adjoining cubicle. (This is particularly true if your geek has a geek boss; see section 1.4.2.) Do not attempt to interfere in this form of geek pairing behavior. Think of two cats grooming each other. Yes, each cat will have to clean its ownself later, but it is the symbolism that counts. However, your geek may not be staying up to bond. Geeks can be very competitive about their sleep, and the ability to go for long periods without it. Like ironman contests, the geek welcomes the chance to show off his endurance and capacity for physical mortification—and not in the service of some dumb triathlon, but for whichever higher purpose your geek is currently engaged in. If you feel your geek is engaging in sleep deprivation merely to one-up another geek,

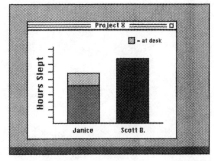

fig. 3.3.3

suggest that she catch forty winks and then be the first one at his desk in the morning, when she will be able to overtake all comers.

3.3.4 Is Your Geek Dormant?

At times you may notice that your geek is sleeping more than usual. Your geek will sleep late, take naps, and sometimes fall asleep when reading or watching a movie. Her usual restlessness will still be seen when she is awake, but be aware that your geek may be in a dormant state. When your geek isn't feeling challenged, she may go into this state in order to store up energy for her next battle. Do not try to talk your geek out of her dormancy. While they are usually quite self-aware, geeks are in extreme denial about dormancy. The idea of a need for regeneration, a time that is not filled with challenges and conflicts is repellent to your geek, even while she indulges in the regeneration process.

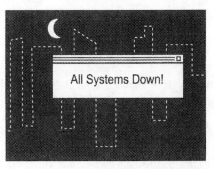

All Systems Down!

fig. 3.3.4

While your geek is dormant, simply make sure she is getting proper nutrition, that she is not actually depressed, and await her next production cycle.

3.4 Your Geek's Moving Parts

3.4.1 Exercise Is Efficient

Could your geek be more robust? Every geek needs some form of physical exercise, although he will resist it with all the tenacity of a Borg drone. Your geek has horrific, traumatizing associations with any form of prescribed physical movement. PE was not a good time for him in school, and the locker room may still haunt his nightmares. Some geeks have included sports in their adult life in the form of on-line fantasy baseball leagues, but generally they are content, even proud, to remain desk jockeys.

Remind your geek of the need for maintenance. It's all the more important in the case of wetware, which has no backup. You've got to tune all moving parts, check motor functions, and protect against breakdowns. Sure, Klingons have internal redundancies (two of every organ)—this is what makes them great warriors. Your geek has to work with the human form he's got. Point out that his work will benefit from a healthy, fit body. Oxygen will flow more efficiently to his brain. A stronger muscular–skeletal system will help guard against fatigue during those all-night coding sessions. Greater flexibility helps with RSI, and strength will come in handy during the inevitable frequent office moves due to buyouts, re-orgs, and the pursuit of cooler employment.

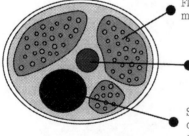

Flexible musculature = longer mousing (more DOOM)

Faster blood flow = quicker thinking and coding

Strong veins = more rapid cleansing of blood and quicker access to fresh blood (see above)

fig. 3.4.1 Exercise is efficient

Some geeks emulate their former torturers and have all-geek basketball or softball games after work with other geeks. While such activities are useful in your geeks socializing process, they generally do not count as exercise in the way that physiologists understand it. (Particularly geek softball, which tends to involve a lot of beer drinking.) Without denigrating the skill level of your geek's fellow athletes, make it clear that these once-a-week activities are only one aspect of an overall fitness program.

Your geek may make the case that the live-action role-playing games he occasionally participates in are excellent exercise. Your response to this should not include derision, or any hint that you might possibly think your geek is nuts. You will never get him to stop playing the RPGs. The thing is to get him to exercise *in addition* to playing the RPGs. Bring up the issue of the World Wrestling Federation. Tell him that they are the only other people you can think of who "exercise" while playing a part and wearing a costume. Does he find them to be strapping examples of humankind? Confronted with this data set, your geek should understand that keeping in shape will not only make him a more effective warrior, it may eliminate the need for swirling capes and robes and open up the possibility of a more formfitting costume to wear at cons. (If your geek's role-playing games are limited to on-line environments, this option may be less attractive.)

3.4.2 The Martial Arts

Geeks enjoy technobattles, but they are not averse to a little hand-to-hand combat if the opportunity presents itself. And if the hand-to-hand combat also includes kicking and weird yelling, so much the better. The mighty Klingons, perhaps the most physical of the future species, may provide inspiration. The Klingons, despite their bird-of-prey ships and superior cloaking devices, still spend a great deal of time maintaining their physical selves with *Mok'bara* and a warrior-calisthenics holodeck program. Though there is not yet a Klingon exercise tape available, your geek can enjoy other activities with similar moves and guttural shouts. Tae kwan do, Tae Bo, and karate all have a mystical vibe and slightly robotic hand movements which will appeal to your geek, and the costumes, with their subtle indications of rank, will also be fun for him. Of course you must guard against geek overenthusiasm and

fig. 3.4.2 Klingon workout (with Batt'leh)

gently remind your geek when and where it is appropriate to do his chops. If you live in a small apartment, be sure to move precious breakables out of the way.

How should you show your geek that you find his prowess astonishing? Looking wide-eyed and appreciative is helpful, but your geek may not require this kind of feedback, as it subtly implies that you are surprised and impressed that he can manage any physical challenges at all. While acknowl-edging any achievements or progress your geek makes (e.g., a move to brown belt), be sure to act as if this merely confirms your faith that, with his superior mindpower, he can accomplish anything. Just think: the Klingon's ferocity matched with the cool logic of the Vulcan! The martial arts of the future hint at this exciting possibility and your geek will respond accordingly.

3.4.3 Equipment Strategies

Anything with a console will appeal to your geek. Look for something as complex as possible, with a variety of displays. Anything that charts your geek's progress over time will go over big. Some exercise machines even have heart rate monitors which your geek straps on to various body parts, though

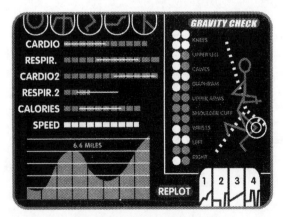

fig. 3.4.3 Equipment with complex displays

if you have seen *Lawnmower Man* this may concern you. Your geek may not know that some gyms have fake rock walls where she can "sim-climb." Next time you are flying, pick up the skymall magazine and check out those self-contained lap pools.

Some gyms offer machines with internet access, designed to appeal to the geek exerciser. This thinking flows from the common misperception that many geeks suffer from a form of attention deficit disorder. Your geek does not lack for attention! She in fact suffers from an abundance of it. Your geek has *so much* attention that she tries to pour it into many active processes at once for fear of overload. Thus, a particular individual activity may suffer from a lack of attention, but the problem overall is one of focus and not of supply.

Your geek needs to learn to enjoy exercise, and spend some time in a rhythm other than the call and response of his E-mail, Instant Messenger, or surf habits. Encourage your geek to learn disconnect, to ignore distraction. Riding an exercise bike and listening to a CD is the equivalent of time in a severe isolation tank for your geek without the trauma of going completely off the grid. The soothing display of the bike, which shows her mph, resistance level, hill profile, and time remaining, provides data but requires nothing from him. Just think, if your geek can learn to resist the call of this display, to see that there is a machine she *does not need to pay attention to*, and enjoy other, off-line behaviors such as the rhythm of the bike and the music, an unconscious breaking free may occur which can affect your geek profoundly in the future. This does not mean, however, that your geek will not, in the end, leap off the bike, grab her cellphone or palmtop, and reassure herself that the link still exists.

3.4.4 Extreme Geeks

A segment of the geek population (generally those in the less hardcore professions, such as content management, Web design, community building) enjoys the trendy "extreme" sports. Snowboarding, bungee jumping, off-road biking, and the like appeal to the rebel within these geeks, providing some kind of physical analog to the thrill of installing Linux or other open source operating systems. While these activities may require going off-line, the need for equipment remains high and the geek may be entranced by the number of new gadgets available. Within reason, extreme sports are acceptable outlets for excess geek adrenaline, but they are no substitute for regular maintenance, and your geek should understand this.

3.5 Common Geek Bugs and Suggestions for Fixes

Even the best-maintained geek will break down sometimes. Some bugs (low blood sugar, a frequent need to play arcade games) can be quickly and easily fixed. Others are much more difficult to diagnose and to treat. Often your geek's major features will continue to function normally and only the most alert owner will recognize the signs indicating an imminent breakdown. These systemic ailments require time and patience and there is never a full recovery. The most you can hope for is to keep any chronic condition(s) under control.

3.5.1 Hoarding

Why geeks cling to their machines, how to tell when hoarding has become excessive, gentle removal suggestions

fig. 3.5.1 Hoarding

Symptoms

Particularly affects coworkers and spouses, occasionally neighbors. Why, you think to yourself, is there so much equipment around? Equipment that is never used? What possible reason could there be for three broken external floppy drives, a monitor that only displays text, and cables which connect a defunct machine to an extinct one?

Background

Geeks need their stuff. These primitive machines connect your geek to a time when he was first discovering computers and the joy of tinkering. Your geek was probably not the most socially advanced child on the block. Sure, he got A's in math, but that doesn't matter in the harsh, cruel value system of the playground. In fact, it's quite likely that it worked against him. Rejected by his peers, your geek found refuge in the machines he could build. Suddenly, his superior mind was an asset, not a liability. He wasn't building a simple machine, but one that he could program and infinitely reconfigure. It weighed sixty pounds and had a screen four inches square, but it was all his.

As his life went on, the computers changed, but their importance in his life only grew. A computer got your geek into college, and it got him his first job. The computer is his lifeline and method of communicating with other geeks. These old, broken, decrepit computers are essential artifacts. Don't try to take them away from him. This will confuse and frighten your geek. "What if *I* break down?" he will think. "Would they just cart me away?"

❗ Management Tips

Hoarding is a deep, almost primal geek behavior. There are many things about your geek that you will be able to change, but this is not one of them. Encourage your geek to get in touch with local schools or non-profits to whom he can donate old equipment. Bargain with your geek. Use his need to upgrade and approve new purchases on the condition that older machines are put out to pasture. Your geek may argue that his older machines and cables are a safety measure for unforeseen emergencies, such as a long-lost relative with a particularly unusual SCSI need. At this point it is time to think about a workshop space, if you don't already have one. Buy more shelving units, pat your geek lovingly, and move on.

3.5.2 Start-up Syndrome:

Why the concept of working twice as
hard for half the money appeals to geeks

Symptoms
Start-up syndrome is a relatively new but
extremely pervasive geek malady.

One day your geek comes home from work
and announces that he and some buddies
are going to launch their own company.
Depending on your geek's role in the new
venture, he then spends the next year or so
coding madly or explaining the project to
possible VC sources. During this time, your
geek has little to no income and even less
time and patience than he did before.

Background
In the geeky old days, your geek would go
to work for a major software corporation, a
university, or a defense contractor. Lifelong
employment stability was virtually guaran-
teed. Then the first wave of geek entrepreneurs changed the industry and the geek
narrative forever. Bill Gates became the man,
and Microsoft, once an upstart, morphed into
an oppressive and ubiquitous force. The second wave of geek entrepreneurs are now

major players in the economy. Geeks no longer crave security and a corner office at the Jet Propulsion Laboratory, but want the thrill of a start-up and the possibility of total autonomy. The geek idea of success and adventure has changed: Technological breakthroughs must be paired with business acumen in a constantly changing market.

Star Trek has mirrored this evolution. In the original series, the Federation was all. The crew of the ship had one loyalty and that was to their diplo-corporate masters. Sure, they had to violate the Prime Directive every now and then, but the bureaucratic bond was never broken. In *The Next Generation*, Jean-Luc and the second *Enterprise* crew were faced with the Borg, against whom the Federation was no help at all. The Borg was always out there, almost attractive in its sparkly mindlessness, assimilating some of the best minds in the universe.

 Finally, in the most recent series *Star Trek: Voyager* and *Star Trek: Deep Space 9*, the crews are on their own. *Voyager* is adrift in a world with no little navigational marks, wondering how to get back home. *Deep Space 9*, no longer in production, was about a lonely outpost, where the crew had to rely on one another and react to constantly shifting alliances throughout the universe. *Voyager* and *Deep Space 9* are, essentially, start-ups. Like the crews of these shows, geeks today feel untethered and yet full of possibility. The geek with start-up syndrome is conditioned to break off on his own, explore uncharted territory, and reap great rewards while making great sacrifices.

3.5.2

Management Tips

Much of your geek's enjoyment of the start-up lies in the thrill of sacrifice, the bonding, and the socially sanctioned long hours. Geek partners sometimes go along with this because of the great monetary rewards a start-up offers. After the IPO, you can worry about getting your geek back to normal, right?

Make sure your geek knows as much as possible about any given start-up before he joins up. Try—really try—to understand what the product or service is. (Asking your geek for a clear one sentence description is good: He probably already has one for the investors.) Never allow your geek to join a start-up without some savings to get by if the funding doesn't come through right away. Remind your geek that start-ups with friends often lead to companies full of former friends.

Every geek has one start-up in him. If you can weather the one, you could be home free. If, however, your geek makes it big and intends to use his money to fund other start-ups, please see section 3.5.5.

3.5.3 Joy Stick Junkie

Whom does he love?

 Symptoms

Primarily affects the geek spouse, though coworkers and immediate family members may also notice the effects of JSJ behavior. Your geek may play games to the exclusion of all other activities, and romance will suffer. Does your geek come home for lunch to check on his SimCity™ operation and barely notice you? Did he just buy an expensive console which will "realistically" mimic the bucking of a spacecraft? Your geek (and you) may have a problem.

Background

For geeks, gaming and productivity are intimately connected. In 1969 Ken Thompson, and later Dennis Ritchie, at Bell Labs began developing UNIX, perhaps the most widely used multiuser operating system in the world. It was originally conceived so that Thompson could play *Space Travel* on his PDP-7. This is just one of the many reasons your geek needs to play.

Other reasons include:

Games, more than anything else, drive upgrades. Keeping up with the latest shooters requires your geek to purchase new hardware and software on a regular basis.

Games are the context for many geek-to-geek relationships.

Games provide measurable results. Your geek can compare his play to others and to his personal best. Your geek may have a chart indicating his time on various levels.

Games are fun.

Mangement Tips

The key to coping with this type of addiction is to extend the fun of gameplay into your relationship. Try making your geek's environment more interactive. Leave him little notes and riddles around the house which will make his household chores more fun. (Think *Myst*.) Stick a rearview mirror on your geek's monitor and do distracting things behind him. If the situation becomes desperate, cover the interior of the house with plastic wrap and tinfoil. Put a sign on the front door announcing that his home has been transformed into ICEMAZE IV. Make up a few rules for the game to make it seem authentic. Put on your Barbarella gear, hide behind an icefloe, and ambush him when he walks in. The key to this game is not to end up in bed immediately: Make the game last a while.

3.5.4 Grrr! The Hostile Geek

Does your geek have issues?
Helping him to express anger

 Symptoms
While geeks are highly opinionated and have little difficulty expressing their heartfelt views on topics such as platform choice, cryptography, and the virtues of an extended keyboard, they often have trouble expressing nongeeky anger and emotions. In fact,

the more the pent-up anger builds, the more vehement your geek's technical opinions may become. If your geek comes home and finds you booting NT on the Linux system he installed and overreacts, it is very likely a sign that something else is troubling him.

Background

Geeks romanticize stress. The thrill of being on deadline, the anxiety of debugging—these are activities your geek enjoys. Thriving under pressure is part of what separates the geek from the nongeek. So when other types of stress kick in, it's hard for your geek to ask for help. When a coworker is requesting a customized spell-check program, the head honchos refuse to institute a company-wide backup procedure, and the local convenience store discontinues his favorite slushie flavor, your geek has nowhere to go with his frustration. Geeks complain to one another about these things, but such conversations often result in one-upmanship and can exacerbate your geek's misery.

Management Tips

Work with your geek to identify stressors and deal with them as they occur, rather than allowing them to build up. Primal scream therapy can work for some geeks, but choose a professional for anything this intense. Some stressors are an inevitable part of life—clueless CEOs, overzealous marketing schmoozers—your geek will never get away from them but he can learn to desensitize himself. Other sections of this book have some great stress relieving exercises, but your geek may need to learn to take control of his environment, to get out of tech support if that makes him crazy, to go to a more research-based company if the marketing folks are his nemesis. However, if your geek's job stress gets so high that he starts his own company, be prepared for a whole new set of problems.

3.5.5 Made-My-First-Million-Already Malaise

When the Ferrari loses its luster

 Symptoms
The bored millionaire geek often begins building elaborate houses or ballooning around the world. Your geek may start a charitable foundation or other nonprofit institution. Rich geeks often become obsessed with the financial market and the rise and fall of various stocks; in the most

extreme cases, a geek with MMFMAM may begin funding new companies.

Background

The occasional ennui your geek may have experienced while on the road to success is nothing compared to the weirdness he may feel when he has actually achieved it. Many geeks remain in deep denial about their success and, after an initial spending spree, continue working long hours and dressing in the shabby clothing of their previous life. Admittedly, this is partially for cred, but it also reflects your geek's deep need to feel useful, be challenged, and fit in with his friends.

NOTE: Made-My-First-Million is a bug in a state of flux. As more geeks develop it, it is likely to be reclassed as a feature.

Management Tips

For your geek, no off-line activity will replace the thrill of coding and eventually she must return to this. Work with your geek to see if she has another project in mind. Many millionaire geeks are very happy doing consulting work. This is a low commitment, high profit activity which allows a geek to tell an entire company what to do, then complain about their incompetence when they fail to execute her orders exactly.

CHAPTER 4:
LIVING IN
A GEEK WORLD

4.1 Planning for the Future

4.1.1 Real Futurists Have Children*

Though geeks will enjoy conceiving and bearing children "the old fashioned way," the newest advances in repro-

---

*The origin of this brilliant phrase is somewhat in dispute. Noted cyberpunk author Bruce Sterling claims to have stolen it from former *Wired* editor-in-chief Kevin Kelly, while Kelly maintains Sterling is the coiner. Kelly does admit he may have planted a seed in Sterling's mind which later bore fruit—clearly real futurists reap what they sow.

ductive technologies will also appeal. For geeks in same-sex relationships, these techniques may provide an exciting way to bypass traditional gender roles as well as biological limitations. Geeks are open to in vitro, surrogacy, and pretty much any method out there, but be careful of a tendency in your geek to bypass ethical questions in favor of the coolest way to spawn. Discuss the consequences of every decision—if your geek begins to speak of "burning the motherhood statement,"* you may need to intervene.

Once your geek has offspring, he or she will be a loving parent (also see section 1.4.4, "Your Geek Parent"). Your geek will be especially excited by the opportunities children

---

*The "motherhood statement" refers to the tendency of science fiction to explore alternatives to traditional procreation and gestation, but to nearly always end up reaffirming the status quo. Subverting the motherhood statement is something of a *Brave New World* scenario.

provide to upgrade and buy more equipment. Expect your geek to have strong opinions about education and to provide many at-home learning experiences, such as robot building and calculating the optimal dog-feeding-frequency algorithm. Encourage your geek to build a treehouse for the kids and get outdoors. This will benefit both geek and child.

Remember that children overload easily, and your geek may not be aware of this. A five hour Playstation marathon is fine for adults—it's not optimal for anyone under twelve. Talk to your children and your geek about boundaries and "time-outs." Setting up an electronic signal works better for geeks than safewords.

4.1.2 Life Extension

Science's most tantalizing possibility is that of escaping death. While he may realize intellectually that this is unlikely in his lifetime, your geek will likely become enamored of various types of longevity producing systems. Cryogenics, computerized life maintenance systems, enzyme therapy, programmatic organ transplant—nothing is too far-out for a geek who has seen the predictive value of science fiction proven over and over again. (This desire to cheat death often goes hand in hand with a reluctance on your geek's part to do basic upkeep on his current body; see Chapter Three for advice on how to deal with this.)

Indulge your geek in fantasies if they seem to ease his mind. Especially if he is not religious, this may be how your geek deals with his fear of death. You can also make some pragmatic suggestions in order to comfort him, such as the option to put his remains into orbit, or to be buried with a beloved CPU. Some geeks haven't realized that stardates can be chiseled onto a tombstone as easily as Earth coordinates, and are happy to have this pointed out.

Here rests R. Geekson

-368195.5 --324916.6

Eureka!

fig. 4.1.2 Stardates on a tombstone

4.2 Your Geek's Lifespan

4.2.1 Programming a Longer Life for Your Geek

You may be concerned about your geek's longevity. Though the evidence is thus far anecdotal, it seems that the hardworking, low nutrition geek lifestyle might significantly contribute toward a statistically shorter life. Lack of sleep is also a significant factor, as it can amplify even tolerable stress levels into overload. Your geek can escape this fate, with your help, by applying the lessons of Chapter Three and emphasizing a life-affirming attitude throughout his daily functions. Inform your geek that studies show powerful immune system boosts as a result of guided mind–body exercises. Your geek may be put off by the organic nature of many affirmations; it is helpful to suggest more suitable ones.

"I am floating in a vast gray-scale space of infinite peace."

"It is not for me to
question my node in
the great system, but to
make the best of the node
in which I find myself."

"I embrace each bug not
as a sign of failure, but as
a learning opportunity.
I honor the bug as a chance
to improve my own
personal code."

4.2.1

"I believe in
a higher power,
and the possibility
of divine backups."

"Like pi,
my life's sequence
is ever-changing
and beautiful
in its manifestation."

4.2.2 Minimizing Your Geek's Risks

Your geek's life is not danger-free. Although your geek may be peaceful, geeks love adventure and risk-taking. The high-tech environments in which many geeks spend time can have hazards which do not produce symptoms until much later in life. Monitor radiation, poor ergonomics, fringe groups, and careless lab techniques are just some of the dangers your geek may not be aware of. History is littered with geeks who died or became ill in the pursuit of knowledge, from Marie Curie to the scientists at Los Alamos. It's important that you discuss risk management with your geek and attempt to keep her as safe as possible.

Ways to Protect Your Geek

> If your geek must work in some kind of boundary-pushing capacity, try to ensure she is in a support or research position, rather than an active agent. For example, the scientists and engineers at NASA are at a lower physical risk than the actual astronauts.

Review the routine safety precautions at your geek's place of work, including everything from fire escapes to any possible chemical exposure.

Casually ask your geek if her research may make her the target of any extreme people or organizations and work with her to develop an awareness of danger. Don't freak your geek out, but remind her not to open packages from strangers.

Use your geek's passion for technology to keep her safe. Surveillance cameras may conflict with her love of privacy, but they can be valuable allies in terms of security. Your geek's beeper and her cellphone will be helpful in emergencies.

Encourage your geek to work on benevolent projects such as environmental research. A pollution-free manufacturing process is just as cool as a supercollider. Well, almost.

4.2.2

4.3 Your Geek's Role in the New Economy

4.3.1 Your Geek and Money

Money makes the world go 'round—and geeks make the money go 'round.

The new economy is increasingly technology driven and your geek must learn to grok* his place in it. With power comes both rewards and responsibility.

Your geek has probably already told you that his earning capacity is at an all-time high. Geeks have rarely been poorly paid, but it is true that the present craze for internet stocks and start-up ventures has been extraordinarily lucrative for geeks. Many geeks are fine with this and feel that it is, indeed, as it should be: Watch your geek for an unhealthy obsession with wealth. Tracking investments is

---

"Grok" is from the Robert A. Heinlein novel *Stranger in a Strange Land*. It is a really cool sounding word and, while not technically Martian, it is from a canonical science fiction text, which makes it pretty damn close. To "grok" something is to comprehend it in its fullness, to drink it in and be one with it. The goal of this book is to help you grok your geek.

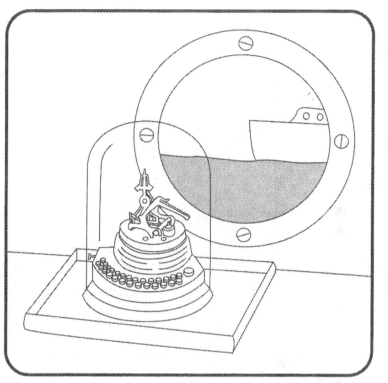

fig. 4.3.1 Insanely great or merely insane?

fine. Taking advantage of an economic boom is fine. A stock ticker in the bathroom of the spare yacht is not insanely great, it is merely insane. Luckily, by the time your geek gets to this point, you'll be able to afford professional intervention.

If your geek coworker's stock options vest before yours do, try to be patient. Feign interest in her various savings and retirement strategies. It's polite, and you might learn something. Your newly wealthy geek neighbor is sure to be generous with his satellite access and private plane, and may eventually acquire so many gadgets that he makes an attractive offer on your home.

4.3.2 Your Geek's Responsibilities

Your geek may feel overwhelmed by his new economic power. Suddenly his lines of code are affecting financial markets and making headlines. Help your geek to maintain a sense of perspective: Encourage him to frequent the usergroups of his company's customers to keep in touch with their needs. Remind him that while the marketing folks might claim the company is legendary, it is probably just a company, and that life will go on whether the IPO floats or fails. If necessary, back this up with statistics about how much of the world's population gets along fine without widgets—therefore the need for a secure widget e-commerce site may not be so dire. Channel some of your geek's excess income into philanthropy—to date Bill Gates has given over one billion dollars to charity.

4.3.3 Geeksploitation: How to Protect Your Geek

Your geek's new economic power makes her a sought-after consumer. Your geek may not be prepared for media and advertisements which target her. Your geek grew up being the butt of commercials and pop culture jokes, and may overrespond to messages which feature her as the hero. Intellectually, your geek knows that after a long day of coding she'd rather play video games than drive an SUV. Emotionally, she may be more easily convinced. Additionally, savvy marketers will play on your geek's love of gadgets and machines by introducing specialized models with complex control panels. Don't underestimate your geek's need to be the first one on the block with a toy that will sit gathering dust in weeks. NOTE: your geek will not appreciate use of the term "toy."

Work with your geek to identify the strategy of pro-geek ad campaigns and discuss his reaction to them. If you suspect the item he claims to need is in fact not mission-critical, remind him of his love for tinkering and the satisfaction of building his own toys rather than purchasing them premade. Do a cost-benefit analysis which contrasts the immediacy of acquisition with the long-term benefits of doing it himself. Suggest your geek make a flow chart with icons representing bragging rights, soldering opportunities, and possible proprietary improvements. These fun activities will far outweigh the immediacy of buying pretty much anything. With luck, your geek may embark on a lifelong project which will occupy him and protect him from further exploitation, though without oversight on your part the project may end up costing more than the initial purchase would have.

Your Geek's Civil Rights

Societies have a history of persecuting those they don't understand, and who is more misunderstood than your geek? When the geek population basically worked for the government, either directly or through defense contracts, they enjoyed relative freedom from harassment. But now, with geeks driving the global economy and geek ingenuity funded independently, prohibitive regulation is attractive to those who would stifle geek culture. Already the FBI has used strong-arm tactics on various hacker and cracker groups, and presented to the public a demonized geek who is to be feared and locked up. Congress and other censorious groups have proposed such legislation as the Communications Decency Act (an attempt to regulate free speech on the internet) and the Clipper Chip, which would provide agents with the capacity to monitor your digital activities.

It's important to realize the distinction geeks make between "hackers" and "crackers." A hacker is very like a geek: one who enjoys

4.3.3

tinkering, coding, games, and electronics. A cracker is one who performs many similar functions with more malicious intent. A hacker might spend all night futzing around with a code to automatically send his friends an E-mail on James T. Kirk's birthday; a cracker might place the same message on the official FBI or Defense Department Website. However, this line is not always so clearcut, and law enforcement is famously unclear on the concept.

It's important for your geek to be active and outspoken on these issues. Urge him to join organizations such as the Electronic Frontier Foundation and Slashdot.org, where he can bond with fellow geeks and lobby for his continued freedom. Encryption will be an exciting issue for your geek, as it pits purported national security issues against the right to make really cool codes. It's very likely your geek will become boring and outspoken on this subject: it should be no problem for him to find other like-minded, long-winded individuals on various mailing lists. It's worth the extra disk space.

4.4 Geek Values Go Global

Increasingly, we live in a world governed by geeks. As geeks become culture leaders, and geek values begin to effect change, what can we look forward to?

4.4.1 Geeks Believe in Tools, Not Rules*

Certain laws are inescapable. Your geek accepts the laws of physics and the strictures of various role-playing games. But within any system, no matter how benevolent, geeks will resist further regulation and seek to find a more idiosyncratic response, preferably one which involves making something. This has led to both a strong libertarian movement in the geek world, and to a proliferation of sub-routines, plug-ins, shareware scripts and bots which individuals can use to customize their worlds rather than forcing others to conform or conforming themselves.

Thus, your geek has no problem with the First Amendment, but finds further legisla-

*The phrase "Tools Not Rules" comes from Cliff Figallo.

tion on the subject distasteful. A geek will instead look to resolve or prevent conflicts technically, perhaps with filters which allow individual citizens or groups to avoid hearing offensive speech, without prohibiting any specific opinions or subjects from being aired. However, being geeks, they will then ignore this option in favor of lengthy and personalized flame wars.

4.4.2 Geeks Believe That Information Is Free, but (Their) Knowledge Is Valuable

The free flow of facts is necessary for your geek to continue his life work. However, your geek likes to get paid and welcomes recognition for his achievements. To the nongeek, there is a conflict here between making all data easy and accessible, and creating mechanisms which protect some forms of knowledge-output. Thus the same geek culture which pushes for stronger electronic copyright legislation and enforcement also urges open standards, shared resources and public access to information.

This paradox may be explained in relation to the large geek ego. It goes something like this: Information and general facts and files should be available to all citizens (your geek may refer to this as "open source"). That way, geeks will be able to write code (your geek may refer to this as "my intellectual property"). In a geek world, the process and its creator are rewarded, while raw data has no street value of its own. This economic viewpoint has an added bonus: It is exciting for your geek to create "intelligent agents" or to think of himself as one.

What's important is the emphasis on individuals seizing upon facts others had disregarded. It doesn't even have to be code. After placing his order at a pizza parlor one day in the late seventies, Nolan Bushnell, founder of Atari and the Androbot line of robots, calculated the average wait time at about fifteen minutes. He realized those fifteen minutes could be profitably spent on arcade games and launched the Pizzatime Theater chain, a franchise which combined pizza and computing in a way geeks had previously only been able to enjoy at home.

Using his own abilities and publically available information, Bushnell was able to create something of value, proving that geek

knowledge is the essential ingredient in any
profitable venture. This equation explains
how geek culture has created both a cracker-
ish love of breaking into secure databases
and an equally strong urge to encrypt even
the most trivial personal information.
(Besides which, security systems are fun
and lucrative to create.)

4.4.3 Geeks Believe in Infinite Networks Populated by Trap Doors and Easter Eggs. Success Is a Matter of Brainpower

For your geek, the world is full of mystery
and puzzles. Life is merely a matter of solving as many of them as you can before you
die. Nearly all geek innovations and inven-
tions derive from this sensibility. In a geek
world, the sense of possibility will be mani-
fest. Geek values will push our culture to
better itself and to rethink its goals and
assumptions. Each day will provide new
quests, upgrade opportunities, and problems
to solve. The difference between work and
fun will be inconsequential, as well as the
line between fantasy and reality. Geeks
know what is real and what is not, but they

refuse to let that distinction limit their imaginations, and they treat their imaginations as blueprints. Geeks do not ask why, but how? Love your geek, and honor all geeks for what they bring to our lives.

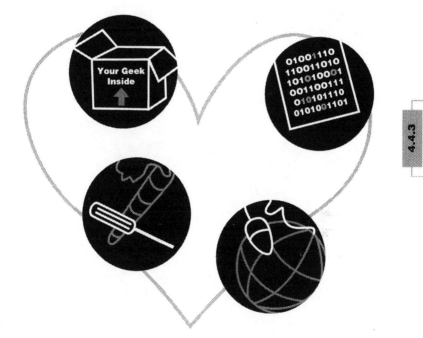

Notes:

Printed in the United States
By Bookmasters